Lulu
the Lifeguard
Fairy

To all water babies

ORCHARD BOOKS
Carmelite House, 50 Victoria Embankment, London EC4Y 0DZ
Orchard Books Australia
Level 17/207 Kent Street, Sydney, NSW 2000
A Paperback Original

First published in 2015 by Orchard Books

HiT entertainment

A CIP catalogue record for this book is available
from the British Library.

ISBN 978 1 40833 949 7

1 3 5 7 9 10 8 6 4 2

Printed and bound by CPI Group (UK) Ltd, Croydon, CR0 4YY

Orchard Books is an imprint of Hachette Children's Group and published by the Watts
Publishing Group Limited, an Hachette UK company.

www.hachette.co.uk

Lulu
the Lifeguard
Fairy

by Daisy Meadows

ORCHARD

www.rainbowmagic.co.uk

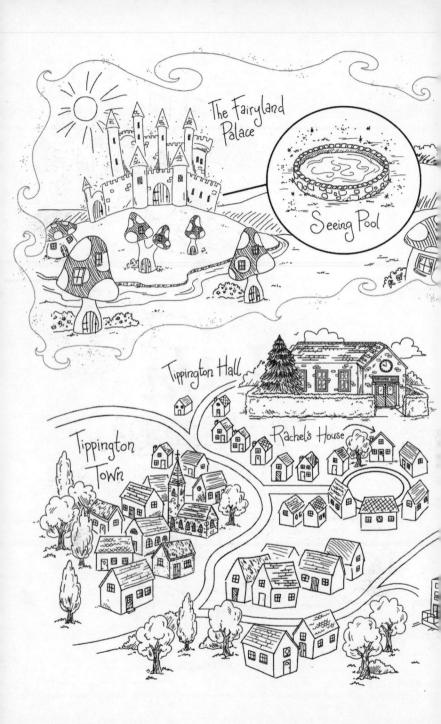

The Fairyland Palace

Seeing Pool

Tippington Hall

Rachel's House

Tippington Town

Jack Frost's Spell

These silly helpful folk I see
Don't know they could be helping me.
But they will fail and I will smirk,
And let the goblins do the work.

I'll show this town I've got some nerve
And claim rewards that I deserve.
The prize on offer will be mine
And I will see the trophy shine!

Contents

Chapter One: Teacher in Trouble   9

Chapter Two: Lulu Arrives   19

Chapter Three: Goblin Island   29

Chapter Four: Chasing the Float   41

Chapter Five: The Great
Moat Race   53

Chapter Six: A Splendid Ceremony 65

Teacher in Trouble

"Finally, I would like to thank my wonderful patients, who have been kind enough to nominate me for this award," said Aunt Lesley. "I look forward to continuing to help them."

On the sofa in the Walkers' sitting room, Kirsty Tate and Rachel Walker clapped with enthusiasm. Kirsty was

visiting her best friend for the spring
half term, and Rachel's Aunt Lesley was
staying there too. She was a respected
local doctor, and the girls had really
enjoyed spending time with her during
the holiday.

"Do you think that
sounds all right,
girls?" asked Aunt
Lesley, looking
nervous. "I feel a
bit silly practising
what I'll say if I
win the award."

Aunt Lesley had been
nominated for the Tippington Helper
of the Year Award. It was a local prize
that rewarded the special people in the
community who had a job helping

others, and the ceremony was that evening at Tippington Town Hall.

"You definitely need to have a speech ready," said Rachel. "You're bound to win!"

"I'm not so sure," said Aunt Lesley with a  laugh. "You've met most of the other nominees. They're all brilliant at their jobs."

Kirsty and Rachel nodded.

"Isobel the firefighter and Colin the paramedic are wonderful," said Rachel.

"And I'm sure Mark the lifeguard is amazing," Kirsty added. "But we want *you* to win!"

Aunt Lesley smiled at them.

"I'm so pleased that I've had your company this week," she said. "You two always seem to be having fun."

Just then, they heard the doorbell ring.

"That must be Bailey," said Rachel, jumping up. "Sorry, Aunt Lesley, but we have to go now. Bailey's mum is taking us all to the local pool."

Bailey was the boy who lived next door. The girls had helped to rescue his kitten, Pushkin, a few days earlier, and his mum was taking them to a swimming lesson as a way of saying thank you. Rachel and Kirsty said goodbye to Aunt Lesley and scooped up their swimming bags as they headed for the door. When they opened it, Bailey

was standing
there with a
big smile on
his face.

"Ready
for our
lesson?" he
asked.

"We can't
wait," said
Kirsty. "Let's go!"

They had a fun ride in
Bailey's mum's car, singing along to
the radio at the tops of their voices.
They arrived at the leisure centre and
dashed to the changing rooms to get
into their swimsuits. Then they went to
join the other children at the shallow
end of the pool.

"Isn't it brilliant that Mark's been nominated for the Tippington Helper of the Year Award?" said a blonde-haired girl in a red swimsuit. "He's such a great swimming teacher – I really think he deserves to win."

"I thought he worked as a lifeguard," said Rachel.

"He takes our lessons too," said the girl with a smile. "He thinks it's really important to learn how to swim."

"He told me that he's seen lots of people who can't swim well get into trouble in the water," said a boy in blue trunks. "Working as a lifeguard was what made him want to learn to teach swimming."

"He sounds great," said Kirsty with a big smile. "I can't wait for the lesson to start!"

Just then, a man wearing red swimming shorts came striding down the poolside towards them. He had a yellow whistle around his neck and grinned at the waiting children.

"OK, everyone, I hope you're feeling energetic!" he said in a booming voice.

"Today I'm going to show you how to do the front crawl. For this stroke you have to think about kicking, paddling and breathing all at the same time. Watch me first and then jump into the pool and we'll all try it together."

He jumped into the shallow end of the pool, but instead of starting to swim, he just thrashed about. Spluttering and shaking, he lurched towards the ladder and hauled himself out of the pool.

"Was that a new stroke?" asked Bailey. "I've never seen it before."

Rachel and Kirsty exchanged a worried glance, and Mark looked embarrassed.

"That wasn't a swimming stroke at all," he said, panting. "I've forgotten how to swim!"

Lulu
Arrives

"I'm so sorry," Mark told the class. "I don't understand what just happened, but I can't take a swimming lesson if I don't trust myself in the water. I'm going to have to cancel the lesson and close the pool. There are no other lifeguards available to take over from me."

Looking very disappointed, the other children in the class wandered over to the bench to collect their towels. Rachel and Kirsty paused and watched Mark sit down on the poolside and put his head in his hands.

"Poor Mark," said Rachel. "What on earth could have made him forget how to swim?"

The others were already walking into the changing rooms. As the girls went to

pick up their towels, Kirsty drew in her
breath sharply.

"Look at your
towel," she
exclaimed.
"It's
glowing!"

"It's
magic," said
Rachel, and
the best friends
shared a happy
smile.

Even though they had been on many
magical adventures, they always felt a
thrill of excitement when they had a visit
from a fairy. Rachel picked up her towel
and saw Lulu the Lifeguard Fairy sitting
cross-legged on the bench.

"Hello, Lulu!" said Rachel. "What are you doing here?"

The little fairy jumped up, fluttering her wings. She was wearing a yellow T-shirt tied up at the front into a knot, a pair of red shorts and pink trainers that matched her whistle.

"I've come to ask for your help," she said, shaking back her shiny brown hair. "I have to find a way to get my magical rescue float back from Jack Frost and his goblins."

On the first day of Kirsty's visit to
Tippington, Martha the Doctor Fairy
had whisked the girls to Fairyland to
meet the other Helping Fairies. Jack
Frost had stolen their magical objects,
and without them the fairies couldn't
help everyday heroes
like Aunt Lesley
do their jobs.

"We'll do
whatever
you need
us to do,"
said Rachel.
"We've helped
Martha, Ariana
and Perrie to get their
magical objects back – and we'll find
yours too."

"Thank you," said Lulu, with a flash of a smile. "Jack Frost only has one magical object left, but he's still trying to win the Tippington Helper of the Year Award and he's still causing trouble."

Jack Frost had ordered his goblins to do the jobs of the award nominees. He thought that he could take the credit for himself and win the award without having to help anyone. After he stole the objects, the people who had been nominated for the award had started behaving very strangely. Isobel the firefighter had stopped being brave, Colin the paramedic had panicked at the sight of a grazed knee and even Aunt Lesley had stopped helping her patients.

So far the girls had managed to get back three of the Helping Fairies' magical objects, and three of the everyday heroes were doing their jobs again and helping others. But Lulu the Lifeguard Fairy was still missing her magical rescue float.

"What sort of trouble is Jack Frost causing?" Kirsty asked.

"All lifeguards everywhere are forgetting how to swim," said Lulu. "They won't be able to help people until the float is back where it belongs."

"Mark, the lifeguard here, has forgotten how to swim too!" said Rachel. "He couldn't understand why – I think he's really upset."

They glanced over to where Mark was still sitting with his head in his hands. Luckily he wasn't paying any attention to the girls, and he hadn't spotted the little fairy perching on the bench.

"It's all because of Jack Frost," Lulu said. "Unless I find my magical rescue float, Mark will never work as a lifeguard again."

"We need to start searching for the float," said Kirsty. "Where shall we start?"

Just then they heard chatter coming from the changing rooms. Mark heard it too – he stood up and cleared his throat.

Lulu darted into Kirsty's swimming bag
as he glanced across at them.

"You'd better go and get changed,
girls," he said. "I'm afraid there will be no
lesson today."

He gave them a sad smile and strode
out of the swimming pool area.

Goblin Island

The girls headed towards the changing room, but just as they went in, Rachel stopped and tilted her head to the side.

"Do you hear something?" she asked. "There's a noise coming from the swimming pool."

Kirsty and Lulu listened too. They heard a faint splashing sound, and a few high-pitched giggles.

"Come on!" Kirsty exclaimed.

They rushed back to the pool and saw three goblins pushing a giant inflatable island into the middle of the water. They were wearing bright green swim trunks, swimming caps and goggles.

"Those naughty goblins!" said Rachel. "We should have guessed they'd be here, trying to do Mark's job."

"They don't look very interested in being lifeguards," said Kirsty.

The goblins were having a wonderful time playing on the inflatable island. It had a soft slide and a hollow to crawl through, painted like a log. Squealing and squawking, they bounced, slid, splashed and skidded around the island.

"At least one of the goblins looks as if he wants to be a lifeguard," said Rachel.

She pointed at a fourth goblin who was busily swimming laps in the pool. Just then, one of the playing goblins slid off into the path of the one who was swimming laps. He lifted his head out of the water.

"Get out of my way, you green nincompoop!" he screeched.

"Oh my goodness, that's not a goblin!" Kirsty said with a gasp. "That's Jack Frost!"

His long beard was dripping with water and had lost all its spikiness.

His hair was slicked back with water.

"I didn't know he was such a good swimmer," said Lulu, poking her head out of Kirsty's swimming bag.

"He's not," Rachel replied with a puzzled frown. "It wasn't very long ago that he was taking swimming lessons from the Little Mermaid at the Tiptop Castle Fairytale Festival. He can't possibly have become an amazing swimmer since then."

The girls moved closer to the pool, and Lulu let out a cry of surprise.

"He's not an amazing swimmer, he's an amazing cheater," she said. "He's using my magical rescue float to help him swim!"

Rachel and Kirsty shared an excited glance. They had found it!

"Now all we have to do is get it back for Lulu," said Kirsty. "Any ideas?"

"I've got one," said Rachel. "But we're going to have to pretend to be goblins!"

Kirsty grinned.

"We've done it before," she said. "And if it helps Lulu, I'm ready."

The girls slipped back into the corridor that led to the changing rooms. Then Lulu fluttered out of the bag and hovered in front of them.

"Are you sure about this?" she asked. "You really want me to turn you into goblins?"

"Definitely," said Rachel with a twinkle in her eyes. "As long as you turn us back again afterwards!"

Lulu laughed and raised her wand as she spoke the words of a spell.

"Make these girls look green and grim, ready for a goblin swim!"

Rachel and Kirsty felt their skin prickling as it grew rough and knobbly. Their hair disappeared, and their noses and ears grew bigger. In green swimsuits, goggles and swimming caps, they looked the same as the goblins frolicking on the inflatable island.

"It's strange to have such big feet!" squawked Rachel, and then put her hand to her throat. "Ooh, I'd forgotten that I would sound like a goblin too!"

Kirsty tried to laugh, but it came out as a high-pitched goblin giggle.

"What do you think we should do next?" she asked.

"We need to get out to the island," said Rachel. "If Jack Frost thinks we're

just ordinary goblins, he won't be
expecting us to try to rescue the float.
Let's play with the other goblins for a
while so he doesn't suspect anything.
Then we'll try to grab the float."

"I'll stay close to you," Lulu
promised.

"Don't let them see
you," Rachel urged
her.

Lulu smiled and
fluttered high into
the air. While
the goblins were
splashing around
the island, she
perched among the
leaves of an inflatable palm tree. Kirsty
took a deep breath.

"Are you nervous?" Rachel asked her.

Kirsty smiled at her best friend.

"A bit," she said. "I've pretended to be a goblin before, but never in the middle of a swimming pool!"

"We'll be fine," said Rachel, squeezing her hand. "After all, we'll be together and we're best friends. We can do anything!"

Chasing the Float

The girls ran out to the pool and dived into the water, then swam towards the island. As they pulled themselves up, dripping wet, the other goblins glared at them.

"There's not enough room on here for two more," he snapped. "Go away."

"You can't boss us about," said Rachel, remembering that she needed to sound as rude as the goblins if she was going to fit in. "We'll do what we want."

The other goblins grumbled under their breath, but they didn't stop Rachel from climbing onto the soft slide. Kirsty crawled through the soft log, and the other goblins didn't pay them any more attention.

Meanwhile, Jack Frost was still swimming laps up and down the pool.

As he came up to the side of the island,
Rachel stood on top of the slide and
dived into the water in front of him.

"I've told you before, you idiot!" Jack
Frost bellowed angrily, treading water
with the float round his middle. "Get out
of my way!"

At that moment, Kirsty jumped into
the water behind him. He turned and
frowned at her.

"Give me that float!" said Kirsty.

"Have you both gone mad?" Jack Frost demanded. "You can't order *me* around!"

Rachel lunged for the float, but he turned and splashed her in the face. Spluttering and coughing, Rachel thrashed around in the water and grabbed the side of the island to steady herself. Then  Kirsty grabbed at the float.

"Oh no you don't!" Jack Frost yelled as her fingertips touched it.

He splashed water in her eyes, and
by the time she could see again he was
already halfway across the pool. She and
Rachel struck out to follow him, but he
quickly reached the ladder
and climbed out of the
pool. Shaking water
from his beard, he
tucked the float
under his arm and
glared at them.

  "I'm going
home to the
Ice Castle," he
shouted, his voice
echoing around the pool
room. "I'm going to have a swim in my
own private moat, and you stupid goblins
are *not* invited!"

Jack Frost pulled his wand from a pocket in his ice-blue swimming trunks. He waved it, and there was a bright-blue flash and a loud bang. Then suddenly he had disappeared, and Rachel and Kirsty were left treading water.

"What can we do now?" Kirsty groaned.

"Follow him, of course!" said Lulu from above them.

She waved her wand, and Rachel and Kirsty rose out of the water, twirling as they transformed from goblins into tiny fairies, now back in their clothes.

The goblins on the inflatable island gave shouts of fury.

"Tricksy fairies!"

"Catch them!"

But as the goblins belly-flopped into the water, Lulu whisked herself and the girls to Fairyland. Still breathless from their swim, they found themselves fluttering above the Ice Castle moat. They could see that Jack Frost had broken the ice to be able to get into the water, and now he was swimming around the moat at top speed. Several goblins were standing on the edge of the moat, watching him and clapping each time he passed.

"I'm faster than a fish!" he shouted to them. "Faster than a dolphin! No one and nothing could be a better swimmer than me!"

Kirsty gave a little gasp.

"I've got an idea," she said. "Oh, I hope this works! Lulu, could you magic up a special swimming trophy – something big and gaudy?"

Lulu smiled and waved her wand. Suddenly a pedestal appeared on the edge of the moat. On top of it stood a large golden cup, studded with sparkling jewels. The goblins noticed it at once, and their mouths dropped open.

"What's that?" one of them cried, darting towards it.

"I want it!" said another.

"I saw it first," said a third goblin.

"It doesn't belong to you," said Kirsty, fluttering down and perching next to the trophy. "It belongs to the winner of the swimming race."

Lulu waved her wand again, and suddenly the edges of the moat were decorated with banners, and a large 'Finish' sign hung above the moat near to the fairies.

"I'm entering the race!" exclaimed one
of the goblins.

"Me too!"
several of the
others cried
out.

They
pressed
around
the trophy,
examining
it so closely that
their noses brushed against it. Jack Frost
climbed out of the moat and came to
gaze at the beautiful trophy. He was still
clutching the float tightly to his chest.

"What swimming race?" he
demanded.

Rachel smiled.

"We're organising a competition to try to win the trophy," she said. "Would you like to enter?"

"Of course I'm entering!" Jack Frost shouted. "What a stupid question!"

The Great
Moat Race

"There's just one condition," said Kirsty. "To make the race fair, you can't use the float."

"Rubbish," said Jack Frost, his hands clenching around the float. "My moat, my rules."

"Yes, but it's our trophy," said Rachel. "And we say that you can't enter with a float. What do the other competitors think?"

All the goblins who wanted to join the race began to nod and complain at the tops of their voices.

"It's not fair!"

"No floats allowed!"

Jack Frost tried to argue, but the fairies
shook their heads
and the goblins
stuck their
fingers in
their ears.
The trophy
glinted in
a ray of
sunlight, and
Jack Frost stared
at it.

"I want that trophy," he grumbled.
"I've got just the right place for it in my
Throne Room."

"It's up to you," said Kirsty. "If you
think you can't win the race without the
float, maybe you shouldn't enter."

"I don't need a silly old float to win!"

Jack Frost erupted. "I can beat the lot of you, with or without the float. I'm the amazing Jack Frost, and I will win, no matter what!"

He looked around and held out the float to the nearest goblin.

"Here, hold this," he ordered. "Look after it while I show the lot of you what a fantastic swimmer I am."

"Now, Lulu!" Kirsty whispered.

As soon as the goblin had taken the float, the Lifeguard Fairy darted forward and knocked it out of his hands. When

she touched it, the
float immediately
shrank to fairy
size. She caught
it and zoomed up
out of reach.

"Hey—" Jack Frost
started to shout, but
Lulu didn't give him the
chance to finish.

"Everyone who wants to join in
the race, on your marks," she said,
raising her whistle to her lips. "Ready,
steady…"

She gave a long, shrill blow on the
whistle and all the goblins jumped into
the moat. There was a lot of squealing
and splashing as they got used to the
freezing water.

"Wait!" Jack yelled. "I wasn't ready!"

He plunged back into the moat, while enormous goblin feet kicked and splashed icy water in his face. Panicking, he flailed about in the water, waving his arms and taking in great mouthfuls of water as he shouted.

"Help! Help!" he bellowed. "Get me out of here! I don't like it any more!"

Without the magical rescue float, he couldn't swim a single stroke. Lulu tucked the float under her arm and dived into the water. She put her arms around Jack Frost and spoke quietly in his ear, calming him down and asking him to lie flat. Then she drew him carefully back to the shallow water.

"You really should learn to swim before you go into deep water," she told him. "You could have been in real trouble then."

Jack Frost coughed up some more moat water and muttered something under his breath.

"Let Lulu help you," said Rachel. "Swimming can be fun as well as being important, you know."

Lulu asked Jack to hold on to the edge of the moat and kick his legs. When he had got the hang of that, she showed him how to paddle his arms through the water to help him to stay afloat.

"You see, you don't need my magical

float to be a good swimmer," she said
in a kind voice. "Just keep practising
and you'll soon get the hang of it. I can
see you'll make a very good swimmer
one day."

"The job of a lifeguard is very
important," said Rachel. "Don't you
think so?"

Jack Frost cleared his throat and
nodded, looking a bit embarrassed.

"I suppose it was … er … probably
quite a good thing that she was here," he
said, jerking his thumb at Lulu.

The fairies shared a smile, and then
heard a loud cheer from the spectator
goblins. Someone had crossed the finish
line. Kirsty picked up the trophy and
presented it to the dripping-wet goblin as
he clambered out of the moat.

"I hereby declare that you are the winner of the Great Moat Race!" she announced.

Everyone burst into applause – everyone, that is, except Jack Frost. He glowered at the winning goblin. But Kirsty whispered to Lulu, and she waved her wand. A scroll of paper appeared in Jack Frost's hands, and he opened it. A huge smile spread across his face.

Swimming Certificate
Awarded to Jack Frost
Swimming Champion of the Future

"It's time for us to go," said Lulu. Among the cheers of the goblins, she gave her wand a little flick, and the girls were caught up in a swirl of rainbow colours. When they could see clearly again, they found that they were in the Throne Room at the Fairyland Palace.

A Splendid Ceremony

Rachel and Kirsty heard the sound of enthusiastic clapping, and then realised that the four Helping Fairies were standing in the Throne Room beside Queen Titania and King Oberon.

"You've done it!" cried Perrie, jumping up and down in excitement.

Ariana and Lulu were smiling from
ear to ear, and Martha threw her arms
around the girls and hugged them.
Queen Titania and King Oberon were
smiling too.

"Thank you from the bottom of
our hearts for all the help you give to
Fairyland," said King Oberon. "We have
something special that we would like to
give you."

Queen Titania stepped forward and
handed a little badge to each of the girls.
The picture on each badge showed two
hands clasped together.

"I hope that these
will remind
you of our
gratitude,"
said the
fairy
queen.
"You are
both always
ready to lend
us a helping
hand whenever we
might need one. Your kindness is always
very much appreciated and never taken
for granted."

67

"It's been such good fun," Rachel replied, pinning on her badge. "We've really enjoyed helping you all."

"We're always happy to help our fairy friends," Kirsty added with a smile. "All you have to do is ask."

The Helping Fairies gathered around them for a big group hug, and then Queen Titania spoke again.

"I think you should be getting back to the human world, girls," she said with a smile. "I believe that you have a ceremony to attend."

Among a fluttering of sparkles, the girls watched as the Throne Room disappeared and was replaced by the tiled walls of the swimming pool. They were human again and back in their swimming costumes, standing beside the

pool. The goblins had vanished. Mark
was standing at the deep end, and as the
girls watched he performed a smooth
dive into the water. Then he swam several
laps up and down the pool, cutting
through the water with great speed and
grace.

"He's remembered how to swim," said
Rachel with a smile.

"Thanks to Lulu," Kirsty added.

Mark saw them and climbed out, smiling.

"I'm glad you're still here, girls," he said. "I don't know what came over me earlier, but everything is back to normal now. Let everyone know that the lesson is going to go ahead after all!"

That evening, Tippington Town Hall was packed with people. The nominees for the Tippington Helper of the Year Award had helped so many people that they could hardly all squeeze in! Kirsty was sitting close to the front with Rachel and her parents, waiting for the mayor to announce the winner. The girls reached for each other's hand as they watched the mayor open a golden envelope. Their hearts were racing.

"I am absolutely delighted to announce that this year's Tippington Helper of the Year Award goes to…Lesley Walker!" she declared. "Many congratulations!"

"YES!" shouted the girls, jumping to their feet.

Looking very pink-cheeked, Aunt Lesley got up to receive her award.

Rachel and Kirsty's hands hurt from clapping so hard! At the end of her thank you speech, she smiled down at the girls and then gazed around the room.

"As grateful as I am, I would like to remind everyone that all everyday heroes are important," she said. "I would like to share this award with the other nominees. Mark the lifeguard, Isobel the firefighter and Colin the paramedic help people every day of their lives, and they deserve this award every bit as much as I do. Please come and join me."

The audience cheered and whistled as the others made their way up to the stage. Aunt Lesley, Mark, Isobel and Colin smiled around at the people they had helped, and Rachel and Kirsty looked down at the special badges that the fairies had given them.

"I'm so happy that we were able to help the fairies get their magical objects back from Jack Frost and his goblins," said Kirsty.

"Me too," said Rachel. "I wonder when we'll have another chance to help them."

"Soon, I hope," said Kirsty. "Helping others feels really good!"

Meet the
Storybook Fairies

Can Rachel and Kirsty help get their new fairy friends'
magical objects back from Jack Frost, before all
their favourite stories are ruined?

www.rainbowmagicbooks.co.uk

**Now it's time for Kirsty and
Rachel to help...**

Alyssa the snow Queen Fairy

Read on for a sneak peek...

"What an icy, grey December this is,"
said Rachel Walker, blowing on her
fingers and shivering. "I'm starting to
wonder if Christmas will ever arrive!"

It was Saturday morning, and Rachel
was in her garden with her best friend,
Kirsty Tate. They had come out to play
a game of ball, but the sleet was getting
heavier. Kirsty shivered too, and buried
her hands deep in her pockets.

"I'm really glad to be staying with you
for the weekend, but I wish the weather
wasn't so horrible," she said.

"We had such lovely things planned,"

said Rachel. "But nature walks and boating on the lake won't be much fun when it's so grey and freezing. It looks as if we'll be spending most of the weekend inside."

"Never mind," said Kirsty, grinning at her friend. "We always have fun when we're together, no matter what we're doing."

"You're right," said Rachel, trying to forget about the dark clouds above.

"Perhaps we should go inside," Kirsty said. "I think it's starting to snow."

"Oh, really?" said Rachel, feeling more cheerful. "Maybe we can go sledging."

"I don't think so," said Kirsty. "I can only see one snowflake."

She pointed up to the single, perfect snowflake. It was spiralling down from the grey sky. The girls watched it land on the edge of a stone birdbath.

"That's funny," said Rachel after a moment. "It's not melting."

Kirsty took a step closer to the birdbath. "I think it's getting bigger," she said.

Read **Alyssa the Snow Queen Fairy** to find out what adventures are in store for Kirsty and Rachel!

Competition!

The Helping Fairies have created a special
competition just for you!

Collect all four books in the Helping Fairies series
and answer the special questions in the back of each one.

Once you have all the answers, take the first letter from
each one and arrange them to spell a secret word!
When you have the answer, go online and enter!

What is the name of Rachel's aunt?

— — — — — —

We will put all the correct entries into a draw and select
a winner to receive a special Rainbow Magic Goody Bag
featuring lots of treats for you and your fairy friends.
You'll also feature in a new Rainbow Magic story!

Enter online now at www.rainbowmagicbooks.co.uk

RAINBOW magic ®

Join in the magic online by signing up
to the Rainbow Magic fan club!

Meet the fairies, play games and
get sneak peeks at the latest books!

There's fairy fun for everyone at

www.rainbowmagicbooks.co.uk

You'll find great activities, competitions, stories and
fairy profiles, and also a special newsletter.

Find a fairy with
your name!